REFLECTIONS

on a Blessed Life

REV. J. DAVID GARY

❀ Created with Vellum

I write this book as a gift to my great grandchildren, Colt and Elizabeth, and any others that God may bless us with. I hope this serves as a bridge to their past and a help in their future. May my life be a source of encouragement and strength to all.

Acknowledgments

First, I thank my wife, Lieu Via, without whose help and constant inspiration, I would not be able to be what I am today. She has been the primary reason I have had a blessed life. Second, I thank John "Chip" Sloan Jr. whose way of teaching, storytelling, and encouragement has been a guiding light. Last of all and most of all, I thank Jesus Christ, my creator, Savior, and sustainer who has given me the courage to put my thought and reflection on paper. "Every good and perfect gift is from above and comes from the Father of lights." *James 1:17*. And God has been so good to me that I am overwhelmed and mystified at the same time.

Chapter 1

Pride Goes Before The Fall

Proverbs 16:18

My junior year in high school, on the playground, I was showing off as boys will do at times. The jungle bars became a contest of sorts. Who could jump out and reach the rung farthest away? I jumped, grabbed the bar with both hands, legs swinging out, hands let go, and the entire length of my body hit the ground. I remember laying there laughing aloud with all the others. I remember having to ask the coach, not once but three times, for the combination to the lock on my locker. I remember waking up the next morning in the hospital, with no recollection of how I got there or what had happened in the time between my asking and the waking. Severe concussion before it was popular to have concussions. I say this to give reason or excuse (both works for me) for not having hardly any recall of my early years. My wife can remember her first grade teacher. I can only very slightly remember my entire grade school. So, I use this concussion as blame and/or excuse for what I write in this unauthorized somewhat fictional autobiography. So, if anything is askew, I have a built-in explanation.

My first recollection of life was when I was in the first grade. I remember having to run and get on the school bus while putting my belt through the loops of my pants. A belt that I did not want to wear and made a complaint about it to those in authority. But my complain went unheeded and thus, I was forced to run and get dressed at the same time.

This is the story of my life. Always running to catch something, something always seemingly out of reach, all the while rejecting, rebelling (mostly in a passive aggressive manner) the very authority and rules which would enable me to catch that which is so elusive.

The second thing I remember is a day which was just wonderful. A day bright with sunshine, with the hope and joy only a 10- or 11-year-old could be equipped to handle. As often was the case, I was assigned to go to the pool hall a few blocks from our house and summon my father to come home. Most likely for the evening meal, but I am not sure. What I remember most vividly is the words of my father as we walked home. He said in words something like this: You are my son; you are a good boy, and I am proud of you. What makes this so memorable is that was the first time and the last time my father spoke words of affirmation to me. I am not saying he never did, but as far as I remember, this was the only time.

What makes this so unusual? At the time, I was not a good boy and was doing nothing to illicit any pride. It was during this time a few of my friends and I were conducting a money-making business. We had discovered that an empty used old pop bottle (soda for those who are uneducated) was worth a penny. So, we had taken to the highways and byways picking up discarded bottles. We could go to the movies for 10 cents, so we scoured the area to find all we could. But the summer in eastern North Carolina was hot and dusty, so we quickly got tired of all the scouring. But what we learned was that a lot of people bought a lot of sodas and would place the empty bottles in their garage or out-building until their next trip to the store. Easy picking for some sharp and quick little boys. So began our criminal enterprise. About that time, we also discovered that the store which was buying our stolen goods, stored the bottles out back of the store waiting for the soda delivery trucks to pick them up. Out of our newfound criminal minds, we began a systematic plan of going to the back of the store, taking as many bottles as we needed for the day, walking around the building, and selling them back to their rightful owner. A stroke of genius on our part. So, it was during this great crime spree my father spoke those life altering words. I don't know if he was suspicious of my activities and just using reverse psychology or if he was just being honest with his feelings. But whatever the motivation, I never stole anymore bottles. Sometimes I believe he did it to gain my attention and he knew what I was doing. Other times it seems I am unsure of his motivation, but feel it somehow was aimed at changing me. Therefore, I have a hard time accepting affirmation, that which I seek most of all, because I am always fearing there is some other motive and their affirmation is insincere at the very roots of it. I am always suspicious of people because I feel everyone wants something from me.

Two other memories that occurred during that same time period: One day I was sitting on the back porch, alone as usual, when I noticed the light bulb which hung from a single wire. I wondered to myself, *What is inside the part the bulb screws into.* So, I grabbed a chair, stood on it to reach the bulb, and proceeded to dismantle the assembly. Once completed, all I had was two bare wires hanging from the ceiling. My curiosity being what it was, I asked myself, *What would happen if I touched these wires together.* So, I grabbed hold of both wires and put them together. Of course, sparks flew, putting the fear in me, and I quickly let go. To my amazement, I put the whole assembly back together and left it as if nothing had ever been touched.

Another day, I was sitting alone (again) and looked over at the 50-gallon drum in which we used to burn our garbage. As my eyes scanned that drum, I also became aware of a gasoline container sitting inside the garage. My mind, sharp as can be, began to form a question, *What would happen if I started to burn some garbage and then throw gasoline into the fire?* A scientific experiment if ever there was one. So, I gathered some garbage and placed it neatly in the drum. Retrieving a pint jar from the back porch, I filled it half full with gasoline. All is well up to this point. But in every experiment, there seems to be a problem. My problem was I could not see down inside the drum unless I stood on a rock and looked over the edge. So, you get the picture. Trash burning in the drum and myself leaning on the drum with my head over the edge. Arms raised and in one great heave, I threw the pint jar in the drum. It was a success. I found out what happens when you throw gas on a fire. I also found out what happens when fire hits your eyebrows, your hair, and other parts of your face.

How I believe this has impacted my life is simply this: My desire to be rebellious, to be adventurous, to get out from inside the lines is dampened by the results of those early attempts to go where I had never gone before. My desire for adventure is often overcome and outvoted by my desire not to fail or get hurt. So, I have in life become a cautious adventurer of sorts, seeking to live a life with one foot inside the line and another just outside of it. Of course, this causes a lot of worry and frustration because of the inability to seek greater things while knowing the normal is never good enough. It is like being tired of vanilla ice cream but not having the courage to try Rocky Road. The Bible says, "A double minded man is unstable in all his ways." A fairly accurate account of my life.

My oldest son wrote a paper for his English class. A paper which could have been written by me, if I had been that smart and talented. It expresses my feelings as a youth, as a grown-up man, and as an old man still trying to find his way. He has given me permission to share this with you.

"Do You Like My Jeans" by Michael Gary, Oct. 2, 1985:

The noise of the people crowding the store wakes me up. I hear the sound of laughing and I look up in time to see another pair of Jordache prance out the door. It's been a long night and by the looks of things, it's going to be a very long day. As usual, though, I'll probably just hang here on the rack all alone while people walk right by me.

I'm not the best-looking thing in the store, but with a name like Wrangler, how good could you be expected to look? I'm dark blue, plain as an empty room, stiff as a board, and pretty dusty. The people in the store isolate me by putting me in the back but close enough to the front where I could still see Jordache. Jordache, of course, was my adversary, who is beautiful. He is light blue with white pinstripes and lots of buttons. I guess being good looking makes you popular because everyone talks to Jordache. He's alright on the surface but his personality reflects arrogance and hatred, and I don't like that.

Wait a minute, here comes somebody now to look at me. It's a kid about my size, 33 x 33. Maybe he'll accept me and take me home. "What's the matter boy, don't you like me?" I hear him whisper to his mother and say that I am not Jordache and he couldn't be seen with me. Jordache's popularity really makes me envious because I don't like to be left out. Sometimes I wish I could be a part of the crowd, but I know I wouldn't be able to live with myself.

"Hey! Hey! Come look at me! I bet I'll fit." It worked, here she comes. She is shaking the dust off me and moving me around. Boy, that feels great. Is she going to try me on. She is! It feels even better be to stretched out and talked to, but wait. Why is she putting me back on the hanger? I fit her great. She doesn't want me because of my looks. Although I fit on the inside, I didn't meet her outside requirements. There she goes, buying a pair of Jordache. I don't understand why these people only look at the outside of things.

I really feel worthless hanging around here because I know that I could be of some worth to somebody. It's times of loneliness like these when I feel that I should just give up on myself. I mean, if people won't accept me for what I really am then what am I supposed to do? They just look at me with a critical eye and pass on by. Won't someone ever like me?

Well, I haven't moved now since lunch and it's almost time to close so I'll get ready to go to sleep. What's this? Oh, just someone else to buy some Jordache. I think I'll watch and laugh as he puts on his show. I wonder why he put them back. Oh, no! He's coming this way and because it's late, I'll try to ignore him and save me some embarrassment.

"Please don't try me on! You'll just end up not liking me and putting me back. Yes, I do fit pretty good but don't look as good as Jordache. You don't want me. What are you doing? Don't put me up here, I'm scared. I've never been this close to the register before. Are you going to buy me? Why, I'm ugly. What? You like the way I fit and you don't care how I look? Great! Take me home."

It's been three days now since I was purchased, and I've already made lots of new friends in this closet. Although there are many different kinds of us on the outside, we seem to have some common ground and we all get along together great. The man shows his love for us by wearing us and we show our love for him by matching and fitting with what he wants. I didn't feel worthy of all this at first, but he cared for me, fit me in, and now I'm willing to do anything he asks. Sometimes I feel like Jordache and don't want to share him with my friends or do what he wants. When I try to do my own thing, I end up getting dirty and worn out. But when I ask him to forgive me, he washes me out, irons me, and puts me back among my friends. We have a great relationship and I have faith that he will keep me by his side forever!

This is the story of my life on so many levels. Growing up, never feeling like I truly fit in. Never feeling like I really belonged even when I was part of a group. I can recall entering into meetings with other management people while working with GE feeling like I was the least in ability of them all. These feelings persisted even after winning Manager of the Year for two years. Feeling of insecurity, of inadequacy, of worthlessness defined my life and still rears its ugly head even today. But like the story, there was someone who took me off the rack of failure and feelings. Someone who came to me, who bought me and took me to be one of his. Who placed me into his family and gave a reason to be joyful. Who guided me and matched me with abilities and the abilities of others. Someone who loves me and has proclaimed a transitional, everlasting, and unconditional love. His name is Jesus. He has rescued me, made me His, and gives me purpose and meaning. Even when I still try to do my own thing, which is sometimes wallowing in self-pity and self-doubt, He is there to encourage, to forgive, to reconcile, and to put me back into the game where He can use me.

So, what does God do with an insecure, inadequate, self-doubting, often rebelling, unworthy person such as I? He calls and equips him to be a Baptist Pastor and Preacher. Who would have thunk it? Only God! And this is my story, from a boy running to catch a bus to a man running to do the will of Almighty God. It is incredible and I take no credit for it at all. So go on this journey with me for a little while.

Chapter 2

How Did I Get Here

Many people have asked how I knew I was "called" to be a preacher/pastor. Many times, I begin with a story of the guy who was asked the same question. His answer: I woke up one Monday morning, didn't want to go to work, and had a hankering for fried chicken. Somewhat funny, but not too accurate. My story begins many years before I finally became a pastor. It began with no desire of my own because I felt unqualified to be a pastor. Reason #1: I don't really like people. My motto early in life was, "A friend in need is a pest." God has worked on me in this area, so now I like some people, but not all. #2: I didn't talk very much. I am really a shy and introvert person unless you give me a platform and a cause to speak about. Idle chitchat was not a gift I possessed. I read at some time the verses in Matthew 12:36-37, "But I say to you that for every idle word men may speak, they will give account of it in the day of judgement. For by your words, you will be justified and by your words, you will be condemned." I still think of these verses from time to time. But again, God has worked on that area. #3: My wife was not very good at playing the piano. Seemed like every preacher I knew had a wife that could play the piano and add to the resumé of the preacher candidate. But she has worked on that and become much better and now plays keyboard also. So, for all my faults, I never once felt qualified or able to fill the role and responsibility of preacher/pastor. To be honest, I still feel that way. So that makes this whole thing a God Thing.

It was probably a normal Sunday at Calvary Baptist Church in Charlotte, North Carolina. I truly don't remember the exact circumstances of this day. Rev. John Sloan, Jr. was pastor and preacher and friend. Everyone called him Bro. Chip. Again, I don't really remember (think of the concussion) but it happened that Bro. Chip asked me a question. A question that would change the entire course of my life. He said the church was wanting to send some people on a mission trip. They had been exploring possibilities and had settled on one. So, he asked if I would be willing to go on this trip: a month-long trip to the country of Togo in West Africa. I almost forgot to mention that the pastor asking me to go also included a statement that I would be traveling with another woman. Going halfway around the world with another woman. A really big request. I was the Baptist Men's Director, and she was the Woman's Missionary Union Director. So, it was a natural fit. Discussions followed: excitement about going to Africa, concern about being gone a month, leaving Lieu Via and the boys to take care of themselves. This was the day before cell phones and internet if you can even picture that. Here is where strange events happen. I tend to believe it was a God Thing. What do I do about my work at GE? It just so happened that I had been supervisor of an accounts payable group. But recently GE had decided to centralize all of that work into one location in Florida. They laid off the four people who worked in my group, moved all the work to Florida, and left me there. Basically, it left me with no work to do, no people to supervise, and no responsibility at all. So, when I asked my boss if I could take four weeks of vacation and go on this trip, his response was something like this: "You're not doing anything anyway, so you have my permission to go." I can't remember how that all worked out because I didn't have four weeks of vacation to take. But somehow it all worked out. So, all the plans were made.

The Tennessee Baptist had a project in Togo that primarily focused on the issue of clean and adequate water. The rains in that area were plentiful for six months, and then six months of drought. So, the project was about building catchment ponds, digging wells, and bringing water to the people. All of which I had no experience or knowledge of doing. But I was willing to travel the thousands of miles, not knowing what I would be doing, but sure I could be of some help.

The trip and the work were a great adventure. With temperatures reaching in excess of 125 degrees each day, being in a strange place with strange people, not much communication with the outside world, no newspapers, no TV, no radio. It was wonderful. But too much to tell in this book.

But here is the answer to the beginning question.

At the end of the work in Togo, we flew back to the United States and had a layover in New York City. Since it was several hours, a friend who lived across the river in New Jersey came and picked us up and gave us a quick tour of New York. When you leave a place that is among the poor of the poorest, when people still live in huts and cook on outdoor fires and enter the world of the rich and famous, it is quite an adjustment. But as we were riding through the city, I heard a voice, a sound. Don't get all weird here. It was not an audible, out loud voice. In my Spirit, in my mind, I heard a voice say, *Dave, I need missionaries in Africa, but I need missionaries here in America too.* And that was all it said. I realized then and there, my calling was not to some exotic far off place, but right here in my home, in my community. I didn't know how or know when or even had an idea what being a missionary would look like in my life, but I understood that being a missionary was simply being on mission with God. Whatever that mission would be. I didn't know until later that it would be as a preacher/pastor working in the local churches.

Years later, that same pastor, Bro. Chip, came to me with another question. Again, it was out of the blue, strange in many ways, and life changing again. He said, "Dave, how would you like to be licensed to preach?" I didn't even know you needed a license! What kind of test do you have to pass? Other questions came to me, but I didn't ask. Why? Because I knew Bro. Chip and trusted him and if he thought I needed to be licensed to preach, even if it never entered my mind, then I would say yes. So, I was licensed by Calvary Baptist Church to preach the gospel of Jesus Christ. And I can surely say, it is the greatest thing I have ever done. To stand before people and proclaim the everlasting, never changing truth of Jesus Christ is the greatest, most amazing thing I have ever done.

And it all began with a trip to a far-off place, a ride thru the big city, and a pastor and friend who had the insight and discernment to see in me, have faith in me, that I did not even know of myself. Years later as my career with GE continued, they finally gave me a position where I had to do some actual work. I was transferred to Charleston, S.C., where I stayed for several years. Then we moved to Concord, N.C., where I managed offices in Raleigh and Greensboro. We had bought a home in Concord with about nine acres, a barn, pasture, and outbuildings. It was the kind of place I had always wanted. We had cows, chickens, and even raised a couple of pigs. Friends had a couple of horses on the property. A big garden every year was a joy. Then I was given the position of Manager of the Charlotte Zone. The job that was the best in our region, one I had always wanted. But God works in mysterious ways. And it was when I had all that I thought I wanted, that little voice spoke again, *Dave, now is the time for you to decide if that commitment you made those many years ago was true. Now is the time I want you to give up all this, your job and anything else and follow me.*

So not knowing what the future would be, I quit my job with GE, entered seminary, and started seeking a church that would allow a man of my age and limited experience to be their pastor. I said yes to following God and have not regretted any of it. It had been a journey like I could never have imagined. As of this writing, the journey continues. Over 25 years of being a pastor, and with many more to come, I pray.

Chapter 3

Do Dreams Come True?

My son, Michael, wrote the following poem on Jan. 30, 1989.

*The innocence of boyhood gleamed in his eyes as he tugged on the old
man's coat. Penny, was the only word the young lad could muster, while
the water, capped, white, high above the silver pool and slashed down,
down with a rhythm that could obscure reality.*

*The only change the old man discovered was generously given over to the
boy who with eyes closed made his wish and tossed the coin high into
the air.*

*Suddenly, he rushed to the side of the pool to see where his dream had
landed. But a cold stillness fell upon his face as the ripples covered the
millions of dreams left behind by other innocent travelers.*

*His dream was still there, though muddled among many and so many
covered by the moss of time. The boy walked away, head down,
questioning, questioning, would HIS dream ever be found.*

WILL HIS DREAM BE FOUND? Do dreams come true? The song writer answers this way, "The answer my friend is blowing in the wind." Or as my departed friend Tom would likely say, "The answer is a definite maybe". In the Gospel of Matthew, chapter 6, Jesus is teaching on earthly things: what you eat, what you drink, what you wear, the type of things necessary in life. And His point: Do not worry about such things. "But seek first the kingdom of God and His right-eousness, and all these things will be added to you." In my humble opinion, these things include our dreams. Will they come true? It greatly depends on the person and the dream.

I have not had many dreams for my life. Too often, I have not sought to achieve much, but just let life carry me along as the wind may take a leaf and blow it whatever way it chooses. I don't advise anyone to be so uninvolved in their life as I seemed to be, but to dream, to plan, to seek the best of what God offers. That is not to say I have had no dreams. I have, and this book is the result of a lifetime of holding that dream in my heart, but up until now not acting on it. Let me start from the beginning.

I have a picture that is etched into my mind. It is a picture of a young boy, sitting on the front porch of his grandparent's home. No shirt, no shoes, nothing but a book in his hand. (He does have pants) My memory, as mudded as it is, recalls the day a traveling library truck came and stopped at the house. And somehow, I was given a book to read. And the picture I see is this boy so concentrated on this book, the outside world has no meaning. I am open to the possibility of having an errant memory of this event, but not to the result of falling in love with books from that day forth. And my dream has always been to be able to write a book. Why has it taken so long. Plenty of reasons, but the major one was fear. Fear none would read the book, most would be critical of the book, and of me. But in my old age, I have come to the conclusion that what others think or say about me does not really matter. It is my dream to write a book. My dream is not that people will read it, but I hope they will. But it was also the fear that I didn't have the resources necessary to accomplish the task. Fear that I lacked the resources of courage, of faith, of encouragement, priority, and perseverance. Dreams seldom die. They just go into the land of "Put-off." Just keep putting it off. One of my favorite episodes of the Andy Griffith Show was the one where this hobo comes to town and teaches Opie how to live off the land. One of the lessons he teaches him is this: "Tomorrow is the best day to do anything. You can do anything tomorrow." Not good advice to follow. Tomorrow is in the land of Put-off. Well, I have against all odds returned my book from that faraway place and am bringing it back to life. Fear is ever present, but the old saying is true: fortune favors the brave.

My other dream, if I can call it a dream, is what I used to say to people. If I could have my dream job, it would be owning a bookstore. But not just a bookstore, but one that specialized in rare and unique books. The kind that most people would not even seek. Therefore, I could spend most of my time alone, just me and my books. Sounds dumb to want a store where you don't want people to enter. But that is the way with dreams. They may begin as one thing and then be transformed into something else. The thing is, I am 74 years old and still find that dream to be present in my life. Once again, it has come to the front, and even now I am looking at a location and a plan to make that dream come true. Will that dream come true? I am still seeking the kingdom of God, and if that dream is a part of it, God will bless me with the fruits of my seeking.

To you, my great grandchildren, I leave this bit of advice and hope. Dream! Dream big! Dream with faith and excitement. But understand this, dreams are never enough. Prayers are seldom enough. Even David had to pick up a sling and stones to go fight Goliath. So put faith to your dreams, put actions to your dreams. The Bible teaches us this: "Be doers of the word and not hearers only." Be doers of your dreams, and not dreamers only. Seek first the Kingdom of God and all these things will be added to you.

Chapter 4

A Journey Down the River

The cloudy and cool summer morning did not dampen the enthusiasm of this group of young and older folks as they rounded the bend to begin a white-water rafting trip down the French Broad River. The group was excited and somewhat anxious, because for the most of us, it was our first plunge into the adventures of river rafting.

After we had assembled, placed our life jackets around us, and given a helmet to wear, (which did not ease my fear in the least), the guides began to give us instructions. First, we would board a bus which would take us to the drop point, another figure of speech which did nothing to settle us down. As we began the ride, the leader described to us the ins and outs of how to use the paddle we would be given. First, we were to keep one hand over the tee end of the paddle at all times. If we held the paddle incorrectly, there was the possibility of the paddle hitting a rock or tree limb and then it would jerk back hitting someone else in the face or another place. If we saw someone without their hand in the proper position, we were to remind them of this rule of safety. Other instructions were given before we could take off on this scenic adventure. Most were geared towards people who would fall out of the raft. I paid close attention. Never stand up in the moving current. There is a likely chance that if you do, your foot would become lodged in the rocks, and the current will continue to pull you down until you are completely under the water. The leader asked if anyone had ever forgotten to let go of the rope when they fell as they were water skiing. I seemed to be the only one who raised their hand. I don't know if that says something of my honesty or my intelligence. If you fall into the water, use your paddle to reach out to the boat and have someone pull you in. If you are too far from the boat, don't panic, just lay back and let the life jacket keep your afloat. Keep both your head and toes out of the water and every-thing will be fine. Easy for him to say. Every raft leader had a 60-foot rope that could be used to throw to you and bring you back to the raft. The river could be unpredictable and danger-ous. Huge rocks jutting out of the water, smaller rocks silently lurking beneath the surface, limbs and other obstacles reaching out to hinder those venturing in their paths all spelled disaster for those who would not or did not follow the advice and instructions of the leaders.

Life is much like the river. Around the bends and turns are dangers seen and unseen. If we are wise, we will listen to the leaders and those giving us instructions, especially the words of God. We should heed the warnings of those who have already been able to navigate the rivers of life. Parents and other adults have already been to the places where you are only beginning to go. They have the experience of both the calm waters and the rapids. Some even have the experience of falling into the water and being saved, not from the dangers but being saved through the dangers. It serves us well to listen to the experience of others and learn from both their successes and their failures.

We got into the raft and began to learn the fine art of

using the paddle. No one had told me that I was to work at this trip. I thought, mistakenly of course, that all I was going to do was to go along for the ride. Just sit in the raft and enjoy the trip. We were told that we would not sit in the raft, but on the side. There were places inside the raft where we could wedge our feet to help keep us from falling over the side. I thought it would have been safer if you could sit inside but what did I know. We were given instructions to listen to the leader. Sometimes he would say, forward, which meant we would paddle the raft with a forward stroke. At other times he would say, back, which meant we would paddle with a backward stroke. Sometimes he would say, hard forward of hard back, which meant to really paddle with all your strength. This instruction was given when the water was really fast, and danger was at hand. Between these commands was the word rest, stop all paddling. The key to success was for all to paddle in unison, to do it together. When we failed to work together, the raft would go in the wrong direction. The leader knew the river and the dangers involved, so he used his paddle to guide the raft through the rocks and around the turns and bends. Once when he gave the command to rest, one of our group was not paying attention and continued to paddle. The problem was that she was paddling in one direction and the leader was paddling in the other. This got us nowhere. Suddenly the leader realized what was happening and began to yell, "Rest, rest."

The lesson is very plain. When we work together, we can safely reach our goal and destinations. Working together lessens the load for each person and lightens the burdens for all. The goal was for all to go down the river. The success depended on everyone working together, in unison. Sometimes it means going forward at a steady pace, sometimes at a furious pace. Sometimes it meant to get forward, we had to move backward. It was a team effort, because if one was going in the opposite direction, it created confusion and additional work for the others. There were also times of rest. Between the paddling, we were to rest and let the river carry us. It was those times when our strength was renewed as we let our minds soak in the beauty of God's creation. We were able to check out the wonders of the creation in the form of rocks, plants, birds, and a variety of dragonflies. It was also a time of using the paddles to splash each other with the water. A time of fun and joy. Life can be a constant struggle either with the currents or sometimes against the currents. In the midst of struggles and work, there must be a time for us to rest. If we fail to find those times of rest and fun, life can overwhelm us. The Psalmist says in Psalms 48:10, "Be still and know that I am God." We all need those times when we are still, when we depend on the Lord to carry us along on His strength and power. Be still and listen to God. Be still and hear the voice of God and feel the presence of God renew and revitalize us because there is much work to be done. We must also allow for times of laughter and fun. Proverbs says, "A cheerful heart is good medicine". We need times of fun, joy, and laughter to renew and restore us. Life is a continual journey, but we must make the time to rest and have some fun.

One section of the river proved to be a source of many of the lessons learned that day. The river flowed around a bend with large rocks on each side. To get through this section we had to start from the left, go around some large rocks, and then cut sharply back to the right and down the other side of two rather big boulders. One of the rafts failed to cut back sharply and ended up lodged between those big rocks. The raft ended up being wedged tightly between these boulders and we paddled to some calm water waiting for them to un- lodge their raft. They tried and tried but could not move it. We watched as they kicked and pulled, tugged, and pushed to no avail. The crew of the "Minnow", as I called it, finally had to get out of the raft and climbed upon the rocks. We were reminded that in all circumstances of life, we have a rock of safety. Jesus is the Rock of our Salvation and when we stand upon that Rock, we are okay. We were also reminded that sometimes we need the help and assistance of others. Finally, two of the other guides left their rafts, their safe place, and went to help. They took their ropes, walked along the shore until they were in a position to throw them a lifeline. Even as Christians, we are sometimes in need of help, or we are in a position to help others. They supplied a rope which was tied to the raft and together they (an example of working in unity) pulled and pushed until the raft was dislodged from the rocks. The ropes continued to hold the raft until all the crew was able to climb aboard to continue their journey. The ropes continued to hold and help the raft until it cleared the dangers and could safely navigate the waters on its own.

It was a great example of what is needed when people are helpless, stranded in the middle of the rushing currents of sin: sickness, loneliness, fear, or any number of other conditions. They need a rock of security and salvation. Jesus is that Rock. People also need others to share their ropes, to throw them a lifeline, and hold that rope until the crisis has passed. Our leader made a very profound statement. He said, "This is not something to get mad about because it can happen and does happen to anyone." Judgmental and condemning attitudes do not save, but ropes of compassion, kindness, and a gentle spirit do. It was unity and teamwork which helped bring them to safety and allowed all of us to continue on this wonderful and exciting adventure. It took time and effort to make the rescue. Effort for those throwing and holding the ropes. Prayers and encouragement from those just watching. We all played a part in this mission. We all rejoiced when it was completed. We were all in it together.

We all started the trip, and we all completed the trip because we worked as a team, each providing instructions and support with the gifts and abilities given to us. It was a wonderful and exciting adventure filled with joy, fun, and excitement. May we all learn from this trip down the French Broad River and use these lessons as we continue on the river of life.

My prayer for each of us is that not only will we use these lessons, but that we share them with others.

Chapter 5

Berry Picking

The alarm went off just as I had planned. Six o'clock is a little early in the morning for a preacher, but I had a mission and I had planned to get out early before it got hot. I stopped for a cup of coffee, considering I normally had three or four, to help get me going. The skies were overcast and gloomy. There was still a trace of fog in the air, left over from the rain which came during the night. I knew the ground and the bushes would be wet, but that did not deter my enthusiasm. I was on my way to pick blackberries from along the side of an isolated and dirt road.

As I traveled the ten miles or so to reach what I had previously seen, my mind began to sense a certain fear. I knew that ticks were more common and dangerous this time of year. The thoughts of being welcomed by some big snake did not ease my misgivings. Other fears seemed to come and go, but I had seen those berries and knew what was there for the picking.

I traveled down that lonely road until I found a place to park. It was just as I had remembered, the bank on the side was filled with ripe, sweet blackberries. I got out of the car, stepped in some mud, grabbed my pail, and began my search. What a find! They were there, ripe and ready for the picking.

I began with those closest to the road. They were easy to reach, and I did not have to get into the briars, get my hands and arms scratched, or get wet from the water still on the leaves. Then I began to notice something. The bigger berries were not out by the road, but up on the top of the bank. To get to those beauties, I would have to climb the bank, wade into the brush, and risk the dangers. I made a decision to conquer my fears, risk the elements, and go for the best ones. Some I could reach but some were just too difficult and stayed beyond my valiant attempts.

It was a wonderful time. The birds were singing, and some wildflowers were in bloom. I continued picking as I walked down the road until I came to a small clearing off to the side. I discovered that by walking a little ways down the clearing and turning back to the right, I could easily get to the top of the bank where the really big ones hung ripe on the bushes. I discovered that someone had blazed this trail before me. Someone had beat down the bushes, trampled the grass, and made it easier for me. Whoever had done this, and I don't know who, had my thanks.

Standing there in that place, feet muddied, pants wet, hand and arms scratched, sweat dripping from my forehead, I realized this was a perfect example of evangelism. Jesus had said "the fields are white unto harvest." These fields, while not white but black (berries), were ripe for harvest. They were ready for the picking. I was indeed reaping where I had not sown, yet the harvest was plentiful.

The harvest came only after I was willing to get up out of my comfortable bed, make myself ready, and go into the field. Sure, there was some danger and risk involved, but what worthwhile endeavor does not contain an element of risk. I had to face my fears and seek after the prize set before me.

Evangelism has a certain amount of danger and fear, but the prize before us is certainly worth it.

Evangelism will only be effective when we are determined to go where the people live. Wild blackberries do not thrive in well-manicured lawns. They live in their own natural habitat. If you want to pick blackberries, you have to go where they live. Evangelism seldom occurs in our well-manicured, neatly preserved churches. To be truly effective in evangelism, we must go to the natural habitat of the lost. We must go to where they live, where they play, and where they thrive. It would have been much easier if I could have set my bucket on the front steps of my house and waited for the berries to come fall into the bucket. Easier, but not very likely.

I noticed two kinds of berries along that road. One was easily in reach, almost asking for someone to reach out and pick them. Others were higher and deeper in the brush, requiring more effort and struggle to reach. I believe that relates to two kinds of people. Some are seeking and searching for God, and all they need is for someone to simply share the message of Jesus with them. They are ready and eager to accept the truth. Others, more deeply hidden in sin and the world, will require more effort, more time, and more prayer to hear and respond to the love of God. Both are valuable to God. Both deserve to hear the good news. Both deserve the opportunity to accept Jesus as Lord and Savior.

I looked down that path I had just walked. A path created by someone who had gone before me. I was reminded of the words of Paul concerning the harvest. Some have the responsibility to plant seeds, some to water, and some to harvest. In all things, it is God which gives the increase. I was thankful for those who have gone before me to prepare the way and thankful that I was allowed to gather the harvest. Evangelism is not a solitary task. It takes some to plant, some to water, and some to gather in the harvest. All are valuable and necessary.

Only by working together, in partnership with God, will the plentiful harvest be reaped.

The field was thick with berries, but my time was short. The morning hours were fast disappearing, yet there was much work to be done. I knew it was time for me to leave. I was saddened by the fact that not all the berries would be gathered. I realized that alone I could not save all of them. What if I were to go back and encourage others to come and join in the harvest? What if I were to tell others of the joys and pleasures I had received from being in the fields? What if many others would join me in gathering the harvest? What a difference that would make.

I left the berries that morning with a feeling of both joy and sadness. Joy in what I had in that bucket beside me, but sadness for what I was leaving behind. As I walked into the house, my berries in hand, I told my wife of the morning adventure. Then I invited her to get up early the next morning and go back to the field with me. The fields were ripe unto harvest, and I needed her help in gathering the harvest.

Some will ask if it was worth the trouble. Were those blackberries worth the trouble of getting up early, getting muddy, wet, scratched, and facing the possible dangers. This winter, when it is freezing and dreary outside, I will sit back in my chair with a bowl of steaming blackberry cobbler topped with a big scoop of vanilla ice cream. I will say to myself, "YES! Yes, it was worth everything I did to enjoy this wonderful treat."

Some question if evangelism is really worth it. Is it worth all the trouble, heartache, pain, and rejection? One day, when we sit in the glory of heaven and hear the Lord Jesus say, "Well done, my good and faithful servant," our hearts will respond, "Yes! Yes, it was worth it all." Dear children, let me share these thoughts from the Bible. Galatians 6:10 says this: "And let us not grow weary while doing good, for in due season we shall reap if we do not lose heart. Therefore, let us do good to all, especially to those who are of the household of faith." The theme is clear. Even in doing good, there is not always an instant reward. Sometimes we give now and receive later. So always keep in mind that patience is a virtue worth developing. Be patient with yourself and with others. Don't grow weary and frustrated when you do what is good, what is right, and what is Godly just because you don't receive blessings immediately. Do what is good, do what is right, do what is Godly simply because they are good, right, and Godly. Leave the rest to Jesus who loves you with an everlasting love.

Chapter 6

The Clematis Vine

The bird feeder is perched on a pole about 4 feet above the ground. It was not an easy task getting that post in the ground. The soil was hard clay with some small rocks mixed in to make digging more difficult. But I did, with a shovel, first removing the grass and then digging the 2-foot-deep hole for the post. After more digging around the 4x4 post, I planted some small Azalea bushes and one Clematis vine. They have been in the ground for several years, maybe 6-7 years now. They have been nourished, fertilized, mulched, and nourished some more. The Azaleas have done fine, full and blooming, covering the bottom section of the post, except for a small area reserved for the Clematis vine. That vine is a whole different story. Each year it would begin to grow, sprouting new leaves and vines, bringing the possibility of climbing up the post and producing big white blooms. Each year produced a new disappointment, although there were signs every now and then that this year would be different.

Each year something happened that stopped the growth and prevented it from becoming what it should be. For several years, it was attacked by the weed-eater, a strange name for something that not only cuts weeds, but anything in its path. The yard man, (we had a yard man, believe it or not) was unaware that the vine had been planted there, thought it was a weed and cut through the heart of it. We were slow and it took some time for us to figure it out. This was not an intentional attack, but simply one that happened out of the unrealization that growth was to be happening there. But even then, it continued to sprout new leaves and the vine would once again take shape, but with little success. Each time it would once again be cut down, it took more and more energy to come back.

We solved that problem by placing some small stakes around the base of vine, making sure the strings of the weed-eater could not reach it. The next spring the vine came to life as usual. This time, we anticipated it would grow to reach the top of the feeder, but once again we were disappointed. It was growing halfway to the top, when one day we discovered it again broken and dangling from the sting which went to the top. It seems that the squirrels were using the string to climb the post to get to the bird feed and in their attempts had broken the vine. The squirrels had not intended to damage the plant, but the vine continued to be halted in its climb to the top. But even then, it continued to survive, if only as a small and stunted vine. It was persistent if nothing else.

One spring we decided to move the vine to a new location, give it a new post on which to climb, and hopefully a better environment for it to grow. I am sure the vine would say thank you if it could. We again went through the routine of digging a hole, placing a 6-foot post in the ground, and removing the grass and weeds from around the post in a circle large enough to plant the vine, some daylilies, and some other plants. We mulched, nourished, and fertilized the ground much the same way as before. Much to my surprise, because we moved it in a time of year which I thought was wrong, the vine flourished and has grown and produced big beautiful white blooms. The only difference: the vine was now in a new location, a new environment.

It is not that the old environment was bad, just that it was not suited for the vine and the vine was not suited for the environment. The place was good for the Azaleas, but not the vine. To enable it to reach its full potential, the vine required a different place in which to grow and thrive.

As I thought of that vine and its life, I began to think of my ministry at First Baptist Church. I was planted here for the purpose of growing the church, helping it to bloom, and reach more of its potential. I was called to the church with a mandate. Over and over in the interview process, the search committee emphasized, "We know if we do not change, we will die." This was said again and again in many ways during the first couple of years here. I believe people were sincere in that belief. So, I came expecting to find an environment which would foster, welcome, and initiate change. But we all know that what we believe and what we do are sometimes not completely compatible. This was brought home clearly when one of the leaders in the church sat in my office and said to me directly: "We said we wanted to change, but we don't, and we will not." The conversation was about their not wanting to change but also their intention of fighting change and not allowing change.

Change has happened in many of the physical and program aspects of the church, but I have not seen a real willingness or evidence of change in the others' spiritual aspects. If blame is to be assessed, then I am willing to accept my share. But it is not blame which I intend to pursue. I only want to give a fair evaluation of the time of my ministry. Years in which the church has seen new life and new growth, only to be cut short or stunted in some way. Ways which I believe to be mostly unintentional, at least I hope so.

Over the years, circumstances and obstacles and the

overall environment has truly been such that neither my potential or the potential of the church has been fully realized. Certainly the potential of leadership has not been achieved because for the most part, the church (at least those in influential places) has not been willing to be led. Perhaps I have not used the right methods or been persistent enough or sought the right counsel. But the fact remains, as one person said in my office just a few weeks ago, "The pastor is not the leader of this church, just an employee." We have tried to make it work, each year brought new growth, new ideas, new programs, and each year something happened to reduce the effects of these. It has not been for a lack of work on my part and the part of the church. Although admittedly, both could have done more. It seems to me that the environment just has not been conducive to allow full growth. The environment has been affected by all of us and all of us has been affected by the environment.

Many years later, years after the interview by the search committee, the words still hold true, "We must change, or we will die." Only this time, I was part of the "we." This time I must change, or I will surely die, even as my ministry at this church has suffered the same fate. God in his graciousness has chosen to uproot me from this place and move me to a new environment. A place where I can once again begin to grow, to produce more leaves, and be a vine that reaches for the top. And He has also given to you the opportunity to begin again by bringing another pastor to this church, one which will fit the environment and help you bloom again in the Kingdom of God.

My Dear children, I wrote this letter to the church as I was preparing to leave. I don't remember if I ever gave it to them, but I hope so. I pastored that church for over 11 years. Good years in many ways, difficult and challenging years in more ways. So, allow me to reflect on the lessons I learned during that time. There was a popular expression some years ago that went like this, "Bloom where you are planted." While that sounds good and has value, it is sometimes difficult and must not be taken as only one possibility in life.

The Book of Ecclesiastes, chapter 3 says, "To everything there is a season, a time for every purpose under heaven." And verse 2 says, "A time to plant, and a time to pluck up." I have used that to define my life. Different season, different times! Times when I was planted one place and times when I was plucked up from that same place. Each time, each place has a purpose of its own. I do not say that I understood the places and times as I was going thru them, but it was always my faith in God that allowed me to be moved from here to there.

What I say to you is this. Sometimes we can become stuck in a place, a time, a career, even a dream. And when we are stuck, sometimes we just fight harder, strive more where we are, when what we need is to trust God, seek God, allow God to give us understanding, wisdom, and patience to guide us. Sometimes we just need to turn loose and let God. I understand that most often being plucked up is difficult, painful, and filled with uncertainty. But my experience tells me that when God is in control, we depend and trust in God, and after the plucking up comes a new time of planting and like the vine, there are new opportunities for growth and blessings.

The writer of Ecclesiastes says this, "He (God, creator God) has made everything beautiful in its time." There is time for everything. God's time is filled with beautiful things, and you are one of those beautiful things.

Chapter 7

Picking Through the Trash

It was a cold February day in New York City as four tourists left the hotel in mid-town Manhattan. The streets were not all that crowded at about 10 in the morning. Looking forward to a day of seeing the many sights of New York, the excited foursome began walking towards their destinations for the day. Three of the four were dressed in normal winter attire, almost passing for natives of the city. But the fourth, being myself, looked unmistakably like a tourist. My clothing consisted of insulated underwear covered by slacks, shirt, and sweater. Over this was a dark blue wool overcoat with a red plaid scarf around my neck. On my head was a bright orange toboggan, borrowed from a fellow traveler. A video camera hung off my shoulder. I could not have been more obvious if I had a sign on my back that said, "Tourist from North Carolina."

We walked to Rockefeller Center, stopping to watch some ice skaters making fluid and fancy movements on the ice. Memories of seeing this sight on television only made this scene come more alive and enchanting. But I had not come to

New York to see the Rockefeller Center. I had only two major, real desires in visiting this grand city. My desire was to visit Central Park and take a ride on the subway to Coney Island. These two sights were all wrapped up in being able to experience the pleasure and joy of eating hotdogs. Some folks would think this is a strange and a somewhat weird fascination, but I have never said I was normal. Hot dogs may not be a delicious delicacy to many, but to me, they are the food of the gods. I could think of nothing more delicious, more tantalizing, than buying a hotdog from one of those street vendors.

We continued to make our way to Central Park, stopping here and there to see the sights. My excitement was building as we began to get closer and closer to the first of my objectives. My heart began to pound, my blood began to race as in the distance I could see the outline of this great wonder of the world. Central Park, an oasis in the middle of pavement, steel, and glass. A haven of rest and peace surrounded by the hustle and bustle of millions of people going this way and that in search of something I knew not of.

We rounded the corner and there it was, suddenly within my reach. On the corner were several of the horse drawn carriages which would carry us in and through the lush acres of the park. My mouth watered as I saw the street vendor standing beside his wagon that held the long sought-after nectar of the infamous hotdog. My excitement must have shown as my friends laughed at my insistence on buying this tasty treat at this early morning hour.

I walked up to the man who was obviously unaware of the treasure he held in his cart. I ordered one of his best dogs, all the way. "One hotdog, all the way, with mustard, sauerkraut, and all the rest," I said excitedly. When he lifted the lid, the steam lofted up and the aroma filled my nostrils. I held it in my hand, wanting to savor the moment. Finally, I let my mouth cover the end and took a bite. It was as good or better than I had imagined. The best hotdog in the world. Hot and juicy, and wonderful. Completely satisfying to the sight and taste. I could have gone home right then and still felt the trip was worth it all.

Walking on air, I moved to the carriages, paid the driver, and climbed aboard for a ride through the park. Each carriage was in itself a work of art, much like the hotdog that still filled my senses with that wonderful pleasure. The horse was decorated to a tee, from the bouquet of flowers on its head to the diaper on its rear. After having our picture taken on the carriage, we began our journey. The clip clop of the horse's feet only added to the sights and sounds that gave us feelings of joy untold. Joggers along the trails, the barren trees, rock formations, birds, and ducks all enhanced the wonder and beauty of the place. Too quickly the ride was over, but the memories will remain forever.

We left the carriages and street vendors to take a leisurely walk down Park Avenue. On one side was Central Park while on the other side were the high-priced apartments with doormen and all. Those places we had seen in the movies and television. Our conversation turned to those expensive and secluded living quarters of the rich and famous. We could not so much as imagine what it must be like to live in such a place. A passing limo added speculation to our conversation.

We were walking along the Central Park side of Park Avenue. I noticed that at various intervals were trash containers, about 4 feet high, made of wire. They contained bottles, cans, papers, and all types of trash. As we passed one of these, I spotted what appeared to be a bouquet of flowers from one of the horse- drawn carriages. On this cold and raw day, I guessed one of the drivers had decided that business was not so good, so he just quit for the day. And having no use for the flowers, he had dumped them in the trash basket.

I slowed to take a closer look and what to my wondering eyes did appear but several carnations in very good condition. Being the romantic I am, all be it a cheap romantic, I looked to make sure my friends were not watching. I bent over into the trash container, separating the flowers, and picked out several of the best carnations from the bunch. Satisfied with my good fortune of finding this gift for my wife, I straightened up and turned to catch up with my wife and friends. As I turned, there standing not three feet from me were two of the most beautiful women I have ever seen. Dressed in full length fur coats, just standing there, watching me.

So, what does a local yokel from North Carolina do when face to face with two women of such class and dignity? Caught in the act of rummaging through the trash, holding carnations in my hand, I was speechless. At least almost speechless because I heard myself say, "Would you ladies like a flower?" To my utter amazement, they reached out and accepted the carnations and said, "Thank You." And walked away. I quickly recovered from this moment and reached back into the trash container and picked out two more carnations. Hurrying, I caught up with the others and offered one to my wife and the other to our friend. I told them the story of what had happened. We all had a good laugh and continued on our walk. But the sight of those two women still causes me to remember the day my heart almost stopped.

My dearest children, beauty is all around us. It can be found in the simplest of things. It can even be found in the trash if we only take the time to stop and look for it. The beauty of those women was not just physical but extended to their grace and their kindness to a stranger who had so little to offer. The greatest beauty is found when we are able to give it away. Give it to enrich and enhance the lives of others. Even if it's something small and of little value. Take the time to look around you today. Take the time to see and to give something that costs you so little. Give a little of yourself to someone who does not expect it but who needs it. Being a romantic does not have to be expensive. It just has to come from the heart.

Jesus said, "It is better to give than to receive." Remember,

For God so loved the world He gave His only Begotten Son, that whosoever believes in Him should not perish, but have everlasting life." God gave His Son to us as a free gift to be accepted by faith and trust in Him. What a beautiful thing that is!

Chapter 8

The Cows

When we moved into our home in Concord, N.C., a man was keeping several cows on part of the land. Later, after the man had moved his cows, we decided that we would like to have a couple of cows of our own. It just so happened that a lady that I worked with had 2 cows she wanted to sell. They were too much for her and her mother to have to feed and water in the winter any longer. They had named them Ginger and Spudett. Ginger was the mother cow and Spudett was her calf.

Mr. Blackwelder said he would go with me and take his trailer to bring the cows back to our home. One Saturday afternoon, we went to get them. Mr. Blackwelder's trailer was about 4 feet wide and 6 feet long.

When we pulled up to the barn and looked at those cows, I didn't know what to think. Ginger looked too big to fit into the trailer, not to mention the calf that was with her. She must have weighed more than a thousand pounds and had big horns on her head. The calf was just a little thing next to her but was still pretty hefty. I didn't think they would fit into the trailer. And the cows were sure they would not fit. They had never been on a trailer before and had no desire to find out what it was like.

Have you ever tried to get your dog to go into someplace he didn't want to go? Well, try that with a thousand-pound cow that has two big horns to tell you "no" with. We tried and tried but she just did not want to get into that little trailer. So, we had an idea. If we could get the calf to go in first, then Ginger would be sure to follow.

We finally looped a rope around the neck of Spudett and pulled her into the trailer. I got around the front of the trailer to hold the rope and keep her from getting out. The others that had joined to help by now were trying to get Ginger to go in. All of a sudden, I heard someone say, "Loosen the rope, loosen the rope". I looked down at Spudett and her tongue was hanging out and she could hardly breathe. I quickly let some of the rope out and she quickly breathed freely again.

We worked and worked until finally we got Ginger and Spudett both into the trailer and set out for what was going to be their new home. We arrived, let them out into the field with several horses we kept for some friends. It was a wonderful sight as they ran down into the pasture making themselves right at home.

The next morning was Sunday. I got out early to check on my new friends, Ginger and Spudett. I thought they would be in the barn, but they were not. I walked down through the pasture a ways but still did not see them. I figured they were down in the tree area at the back of the field, but it was getting time to get ready for church, so I decided to look for them later.

After church and lunch, I went again to see how my cows were getting along. But they were not at the barn, and I could not see them in the pasture. I looked in the trees but did not see them there either. So, I looked down at the creek and they were not there. I couldn't find them anywhere. Mr. Blackwelder and his sons came by to check on his cows and I told him that I could not find my cows. He said they were probably over in the big bunch of cedar trees and went to see if he was right. Around 30 minutes later they came and told me they had not found them either, but they found where they had crossed the fence. It was way back in the farthest corner, and they had jumped the fence, not went through it but over it.

My wife and I set out to see if we could find our lost cows. They had to be in the area and maybe just could not find their way home. We tried to follow the tracks, like in the old cowboy movies. Problem was, we didn't know which way the tracks were headed, which way was the toe and which way was the heel? Tracks went just so far and then stopped. Up and down this field we went, following tracks this way and then that way and each time they just disappeared.

It was beginning to get late, even dark, and we still had not found our lost cows. I was walking down the fence row and it was as if someone was watching me. I turned around and there standing only about six feet from the fence was Ginger and Spudett. Just looking at me as if to say, "What are you doing?" Not exactly laughing at me, but I could not be sure they were not.

Well, I had found my cows, but how was I going to get them back into the pasture? I could not just ask them to jump back over the fence. I had an idea. All we had to do was cut a hole in the fence and get them to go through the opening and them repair the fence. I told my son, who had joined the hunt, to run up to the barn, get some hay, and bring back to use as a lure to get them to go through the fence. Smart idea, wasn't it?

It worked, well, almost. Ginger, the mother cow, went right through the fence. Spudett, the calf, went halfway and then turned and ran in the opposite direction back to the other side and up the fence row she went. So now we have Ginger on one side of the fence and Spudett on the other side and it is dark by this time, pitch dark as they say. Oh, and I forgot to mention these two cows are black! And they had never been separated from one another. So, we began trying to herd a black cow in the dark back to the opening in the fence that we could not see. Yes, use your own imagination to see this play out! Not too good!

We continued to try and bring those cows home. But they were not obedient and would not harken to our call. So, about the third day, I asked the prior owner if she would come and help us bring the cows into the fenced areas. That day after work, she came, and we walked about halfway down into the field. She stopped, called out the names of the cow, gave a whistle, and stood there for a couple of minutes. To my great surprise, the cows came walking out of the trees, back into their home fields, and walked all the way up to us. So simple, yet so difficult for me. I wanted to shoot them then and there. Not really. All is well that ends well. And we lived together for a number of years, and they even gave us some grand cows.

In life, my dearest children, we all are on a journey. We don't always know where that journey will take us or when there will be a drastic change. These cows were on a journey, a journey to a new place where the grass was green and the steam flowed, the people were good to them. Like us, their journey began when they could no longer stay in the place they were. They were going somewhere. It was not a time of their choosing, or a place of their choosing. But they were going somewhere. The writer of Ecclesiastes said, "To everything there is a season, a time for every purpose under heaven. A time to be born and a time to die." Birth and death are all a part of the human experience, a part of our journey which begins at birth, but ends at death. And we do not get to choose either. But based on the word of God, we get to choose our final destination. We get to choose the place of our ending journey. Jesus said to a man seeking to know about his journey, "For God so loved the world he gave His only Begotten Son, that whosoever believes in Him should not perish but have everlasting life. For God did not send His Son into the world to condemn the world, but that the world through Him might be saved. He who believes in Him is not condemned, but he who does not believe is condemned already, because he has not believed in the name of the only Begotten Son of God." We can either choose Jesus and receive everlasting life in a place called heaven or we cannot choose Jesus and be condemned for all eternity. Birth and death, we have not choice over when and where. But the choice of where we spend eternity is ours. I pray you choose Jesus.

Chapter 9

My Prayer

My dearest great grandchildren, as I write these words, you are both around the age of 2 and act like typical two-year-olds which makes me glad for your visits but happy when you leave. This may sound harsh, but you will understand better if you have children of your own. You are both special and wonderful in your own way. And I never knew I could love more than my children until Dylan, McKenzie, Taylor, Matthew, Ryan, and Maria came along. And I never knew I could love even more until you both came along. It is such a joy just to watch you.

The Apostle Paul writes to the church of the Thessalonians, "We give thanks to God always for you all, making mention of you in our prayers, remembering without ceasing your work of faith, labor of love, and patience of hope in our Lord Jesus Christ in the sight of our God and Father."

That is my prayer for you both. That your work, your life's work, whatever it may be, will be a work of faith. That faith is God, the faith and trust that God will direct you, protect you, and provide for you will be the foundation and rock upon which your decisions and vocations are made. May your life's work be a reflection of your faith in God and in yourself. May it be a labor of love. Not only a love for the work, but a love for God and for others. God gave us the two great commandments: Love God--Love Your Neighbor. May your life be blessed by the love of others and may you be a blessing by loving others. May your life always be colored by a hope in God. An assurance that God is able to do above all that we can think or imagine. The assurance that He who began a good work in you will complete it in Jesus Christ. Know this: Life is not always good, troubles sometimes come, but be patience for God is working all things out, God is in control.

Paul reminds the church at Corinth, "And now abides faith, hope, and love, these three, But the greatest of these is love." Always remember, you are loved. And the best you can give another is love.

My prayer for you: Faith, Hope and Love in abundance, received by you and given by you.